We're Back!

A DINOSAUR'S STORY

Hi, my name is Rex.

by

Hudson Talbott

Crown Publishers, Inc., New York

Library of Congress Cataloging-in-Publication Data
Talbott, Hudson. We're back! A dinosaur's story.
Summary: Creatures from prehistoric time travel to the twentieth century and create excitement at the
Museum of Natural History in New York. [1. Prehistoric animals—Fiction] I. Title.
PZ7.T153We 1987 [Fic] 87-5355
ISBN 0-517-56599-4

10 9 8 7 6 5 4 3 2

One day as I was beginning a little afternoon snack, I noticed a small but tasty-looking creature approaching me.

"Hi there, sir," he began, "my name is Vorb and I'm with Mega-Mind, Inc. We're test-marketing a new ultra-megavitamin on your planet. It's called… Brain Grain!

I would have caught him if he hadn't been showering me with Brain Grain. Little did I know that my life would never be the same.

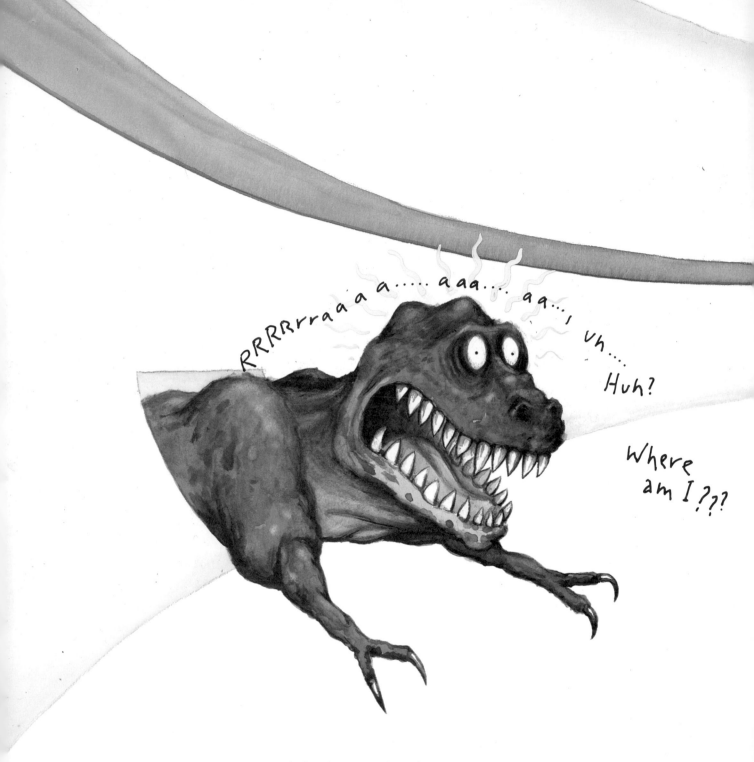

A weird feeling jolted me. I began to utter
strange but somehow meaningful sounds!

"As I was saying," Vorb panted.
"We're testing a new Mega-Mind product and for
the lucky volunteers there's an extra special bonus prize!"
I wondered what he meant. Then he added,
"*And* free snacks." I said yes.

The other folks on board were surprisingly
friendly considering my years of terrorizing them.
I was amazed at how easily they accepted the new
"me." It wasn't long before we became a new "us."

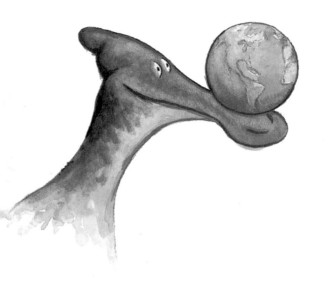

Together we studied
geography, math, penmanship,
reading, and all sorts of things.
Then one day Vorb came in and announced…

"You've passed! Thanks to you all, our research has been a success. And now for your *prize!* It's a trip to the twentieth century! There you'll meet *our* favorite contact person, Dr. Miriam Bleeb of the Museum of Natural History! What an adventure awaits you! Just *getting* to the Museum should be the thrill of a lifetime!"

"Thrill of a lifetime?" I asked.

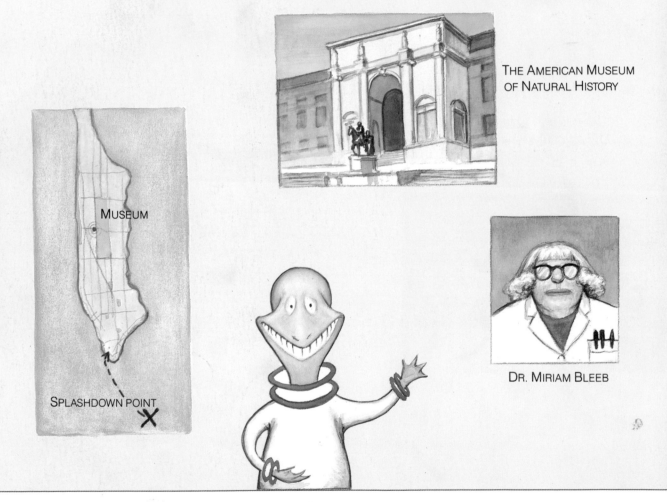

THE AMERICAN MUSEUM OF NATURAL HISTORY

MUSEUM

SPLASHDOWN POINT

DR. MIRIAM BLEEB

But before there was time for Vorb to reply, we were suddenly plunging downward in the dark toward water.

We all sat in silence as we putt-putted toward
our destiny, wondering what sort of welcome we
would receive.

"Excuse us, sir," we asked of the first little creature we saw. "Could you tell us how to get to the Museum of Natural History?"

"You're looking for the start of the parade? Just keep heading uptown. Traffic's light 'cause it's a holiday. Great costumes!" he said.

Costumes? Parade? Well, we didn't
want to seem like out-of-towners so we
nodded, thanked him, and marched on.
We walked and walked until someone
waved at us and shouted, "Quick!
Get in line behind the Wichita Falls
Marching Band! They're about to start!"

Perhaps this is some kind
of welcoming ceremony, we thought.
The crowd loved us! But they did call out
curious questions such as, "Where are the
motors?" and, "How many guys are in there?"
We simply smiled and waved and acted
as if we knew what they were talking about.

Suddenly, I caught sight of what I thought was a familiar face.

"Say, isn't that old Worgul?" I exclaimed. "That allosaurus who used to hang out by the tar pool! Maybe he can tell us where to get a bite around here."

That was my first mistake…

PANIC STRUCK!
WAIT!
PLEASE!
EXCUSE ME
I, uh...
They're rr. REAL!
EEEEEKK
Let's get out of here!

They didn't understand us.

Somehow we found
our way to the Museum.
And not a moment too soon.

"May we come in?" I said, as Dr. Bleeb opened the door.
"Sure, but hurry!" replied Dr. Bleeb. "I have a plan, but
we'll have to act quickly. I can't hold them off for long."

"Now listen carefully. I want you to act like dinosaurs. That shouldn't be too hard," she said, kneeling down and baring her teeth. "Like this. And when I say freeze, hold perfectly still!"

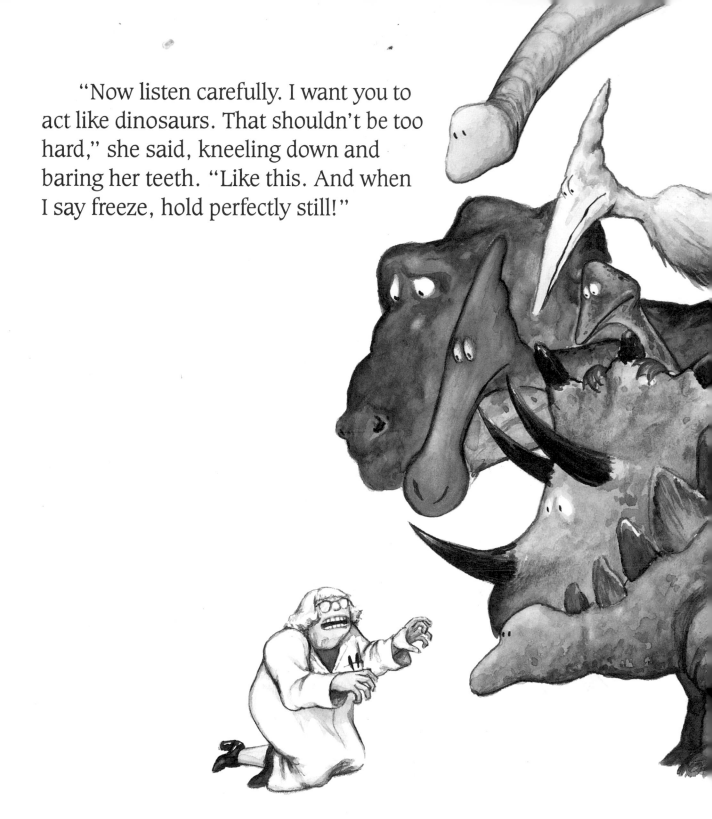

As she got up from her demonstration, we timidly tried to imitate her pose. She hurried toward the door, then turned and yelled "FREEZE!"

The door creaked open and the stomp of combat boots echoed throughout the halls. We didn't move a muscle.

"So you see, officer," I heard Dr. Bleeb say, "the only beasts we have are these models in our diorama.

Mesozoic era: 225–65 million years ago

The creatures you speak
of have been extinct for
a hundred million years.
I don't know who you saw run in here. Perhaps it was
a publicity stunt for some movie or the *Enquirer*."

"They probably went out this way. Come back and see us again when you have more time. Yes, I'm sure you like dinosaurs—you were only doing your job. I must go now. Good-bye and good luck."

"Dr. Bleeb," I said. "Thank you for saving us. But is it too late to get out of this bonus prize?"

"Not having a good time?" she replied. "Aren't you just a *little* curious about this new world? There's so much to learn from each other if you could stay a while, and work with us here at the Museum. But you don't have to decide right now. Why don't you sleep on it. We've got your beds all made."

After we were settled in, Dr. Bleeb opened a book.
"Once upon a time," she read, "in the early Paleozoic
era, there was a little trilobite who wanted more than
anything to walk on land...."
"Go for it," I muttered. We've come this far, why not?